D0243841

THIS BOOK BELONGS TO

· ·

First published 1989 by Walker Books Ltd
87 Vauxhall Walk, London SE11 5HJ

This edition published 2006

10 9

© 1989 Jill Murphy

The right of Jill Murphy to be identified as author/illustrator of this work
has been asserted by her in accordance with the Copyright, Designs and Patents Act 1988

This book has been typeset in Monotype Bembo

Printed in China

British Library Cataloguing in Publication Data: a catalogue record for this book
is available from the British Library

ISBN 978-1-84428-526-6

www.walker.co.uk

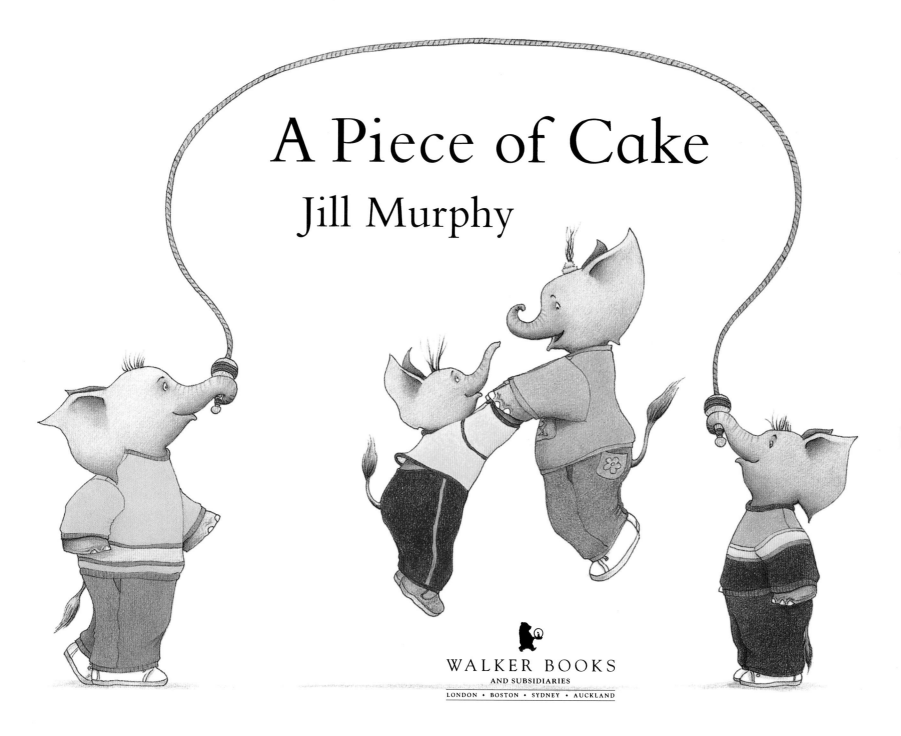

A Piece of Cake

Jill Murphy

WALKER BOOKS

AND SUBSIDIARIES

LONDON • BOSTON • SYDNEY • AUCKLAND

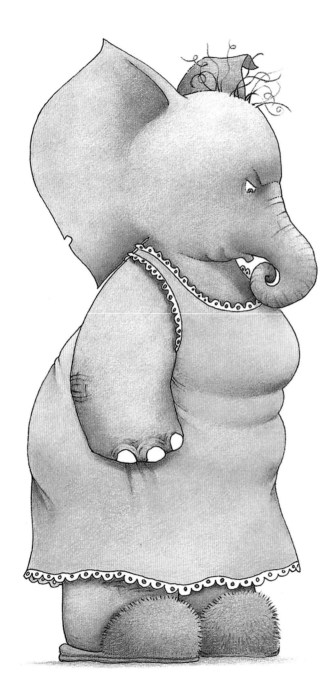

"I'm fat," said Mrs Large.

"No you're not," said Lester.

"You're our cuddly mummy,"
said Laura.

"You're *just* right," said Luke.

"Mummy's got wobbly bits,"
said the baby.

"Exactly," said Mrs Large. "As I was
saying – I'm fat."

"We must all go on a diet," said Mrs Large.
"No more cakes. No more biscuits. No more
crisps. No more sitting around all day.
From now on, it's healthy living."

"Can we watch TV?" asked Lester, as they trooped in from school.

"Certainly not!" said Mrs Large. "We're all off for a nice healthy jog round the park."

And they were.

"What's for tea, Mum?" asked Laura
when they arrived home.

"Some nice healthy watercress soup," said
Mrs Large. "Followed by a nice healthy cup
of water."

"Oh!" said Laura. "That sounds . . . nice."

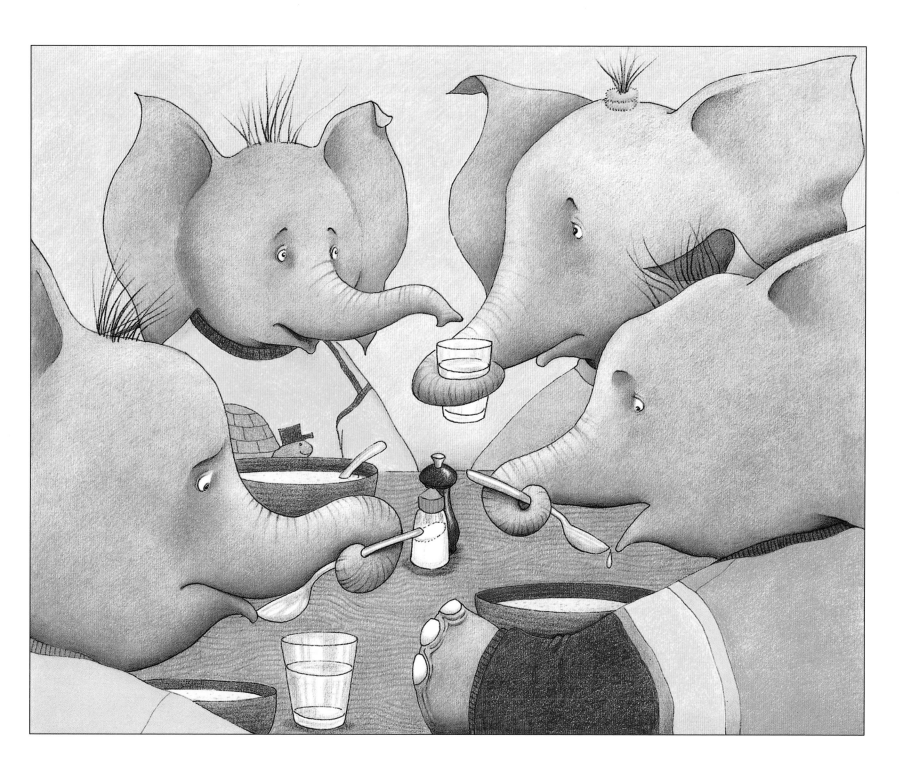

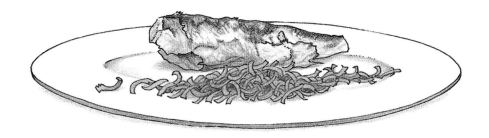

"I'm just going to watch the news, dear,"
said Mr Large when he came home from work.
"No you're not, dear," said Mrs Large.
"You're off for a nice healthy jog round
the park, followed by your tea – a delicious
sardine with grated carrot."
"I can't wait," said Mr Large.

It was awful. Every morning there was a healthy breakfast followed by exercises. Then there was a healthy tea followed by a healthy jog.
By the time evening came everyone felt terrible.

"We aren't getting any thinner, dear,"
said Mr Large.

"Perhaps elephants are *meant* to be fat,"
said Luke.

"Nonsense!" said Mrs Large. "We mustn't
give up now."

"Wibbly-wobbly, wibbly-wobbly," went
the baby.

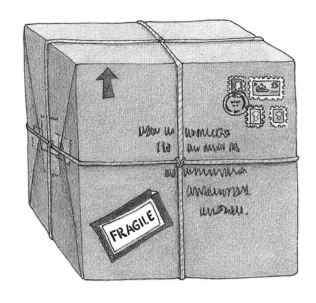

One morning a parcel arrived. It was a cake from Granny. Everyone stared at it hopefully. Mrs Large put it into the cupboard on a high shelf. "Just in case we have visitors," she said sternly.

Everyone kept thinking about the cake. They thought about it during tea. They thought about it during the healthy jog. They thought about it in bed that night. Mrs Large sat up. "I can't stand it any more," she said to herself. "I must have a piece of that cake."

Mrs Large crept out of bed and went
downstairs to the kitchen. She took a knife
out of the drawer and opened the cupboard.
There was only one piece of cake left!

"Ah ha!" said Mr Large, seeing the knife.
"Caught in the act!"
  Mrs Large switched on the light and saw
  Mr Large and all the children hiding
  under the table.
"There *is* one piece left," said Laura in
  a helpful way.

Mrs Large began to laugh. "We're all as bad as each other!" she said, eating the last piece of cake before anyone else did.

"I do think elephants are meant to be fat," said Luke.

"I think you're probably right, dear," said Mrs Large.

"Wibbly-wobbly, wibbly-wobbly!" went the baby.

WALKER BOOKS BY JILL MURPHY

★ THE LAST NOO-NOO
WINNER OF THE SMARTIES BOOK PRIZE, 0–5 YEARS CATEGORY • WINNER OF THE SHEFFIELD CHILDREN'S BOOK AWARD

ALL FOR ONE

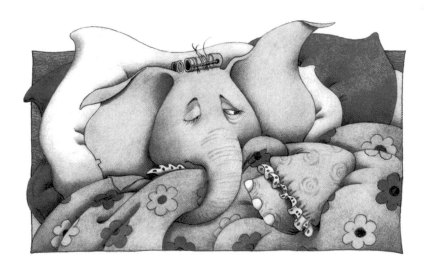

★ FIVE MINUTES' PEACE
BEST BOOKS FOR BABIES AWARD

★ ALL IN ONE PIECE
HIGHLY COMMENDED FOR THE KATE GREENAWAY MEDAL

A PIECE OF CAKE • A QUIET NIGHT IN • MR LARGE IN CHARGE

THE LARGE FAMILY COLLECTION